D0350863

WARNING! DO NOT USE YOUR REAL NAME!

"ONLY AN IDIOT BELIEVES THAT HE CAN
WRITE THE TRUTH ABOUT HIMSELF."
— ERIC AMBLER,
HERE LIES : AN AUTOBIOGRAPHY

A NOTE ON THE ART

Longtime readers and fans of small print know that this is where I talk about ink.
So let's talk! We only used three colors to print this book: red, black, and orangey-
yellow. That means that everything in the pictures, no matter what color it is in real
life, or what color I say it is in the text, will appear red, black, or orangey-yellow.
Or white, of course, which is the color of the paper we print these books on.
There's a video game character called RED SPY in this book. In the pictures, he's
red! There's also a character called BLUE SPY. In the pictures, he's orangey-yellow!
We know about blue ink. In fact, we could have used as many colors as we wanted
to print these books. We just didn't want to. We think the limited color palette
lends these books panache. We hope you agree! If you don't, you can send Mike
Lowery, the illustrator, a letter c/o our publisher at the address below. And while
I am sure he will read your letter with great interest, I should warn you: When the
next Mac B. Kid Spy comes out, we're just going to use a few colors again. We
can be very stubborn about inks.

—M.B.

For Julia, Pete, Ottie, and Bea.
—M.B.

To Brandon, Caleb, Josh, and the other Josh.
—M.L.

Text copyright © 2020 by Mac Barnett • Illustrations copyright © 2020 by Mike Lowery
All rights reserved. Published by Orchard Books, an imprint of Scholastic Inc., *Publishers since 1920.*
ORCHARD BOOKS and design are registered trademarks of Watts Publishing Group, Ltd., used under license.
SCHOLASTIC and associated logos are trademarks and/or registered trademarks of Scholastic Inc. • Game
Boy is a registered trademark of Nintendo Co. Ltd. • The publisher does not have any control over and
does not assume any responsibility for author or third-party websites or their content. • No part of this
publication may be reproduced, stored in a retrieval system, or transmitted in any form or by any means,
electronic, mechanical, photocopying, recording, or otherwise, without written permission of the publisher.
For information regarding permission, write to Scholastic Inc., Attention: Permissions Department, 557
Broadway, New York, NY 10012. • This book is a work of fiction. Names, characters, places, and incidents
are either the product of the author's imagination or are used fictitiously, and any resemblance to actual
persons, living or dead, business establishments, events, or locales is entirely coincidental.
Library of Congress Cataloging-in-Publication Data available
ISBN 978-1-338-59423-2
10 9 8 7 6 5 4 3 2 1   20 21 22 23 24
Printed in China   62 • First edition, January 2020
The text type was set in Twentieth Century.
The display type was hand-lettered by Mike Lowery.
Book design by Doan Buu

MY NAME IS MAC BARNETT.
I AM AN AUTHOR. BUT
BEFORE I WAS AN
AUTHOR, I WAS A KID.
AND WHEN I WAS A
KID, I WAS A (SPY).

AN AUTHOR'S JOB IS TO
MAKE UP STORIES. BUT
THE STORY YOU ARE
ABOUT TO READ IS TRUE.

THIS ACTUALLY HAPPENED
TO ME.

Chapter One: Game Boy 1

Chapter Two: London Calling 13

Chapter Three: Knight of Old 17

Chapter Four: Tradecraft 27

Chapter Five: Drubbalubba 33

Chapter Six: A Reckless Spy 35

Chapter Seven: Between You and Me 39

Chapter Eight: Paperwork 41

Chapter Nine: Escape 45

Chapter Ten: A Spy in the Night 49

Chapter Eleven: Guard Dog 53

Chapter Twelve: Dead Drop 57

Chapter Thirteen: Cryptic Message 63

Chapter Fourteen: Rogue Agent 65

Chapter Fifteen: Emperor of France 67

Chapter Sixteen: Passphrase 69

Chapter Seventeen: Red Herring 73

Chapter Eighteen: Boggled 77

Chapter Nineteen: A Favor 81

Chapter Twenty: Peace Everywhere 83

Chapter Twenty-One: Bathroom Talk 89

Chapter Twenty-Two: Anagrams   93

Chapter Twenty-Three: Had I Ever Heard of a Company Called Nintendo?   95

Chapter Twenty-Four: Leave Luck to Heaven   97

Chapter Twenty-Five: Napoleonic Code   105

Chapter Twenty-Six: Actually   107

Chapter Twenty-Seven: Disguise   109

Chapter Twenty-Eight: SPY MASTER: BATTLE EDITION   111

Chapter Twenty-Nine: More Paperwork   117

Chapter Thirty: OK . . .   121

Chapter Thirty-One: Live Drop   123

Chapter Thirty-Two: A New Low   131

Chapter Thirty-Three: Game Time   135

Chapter Thirty-Four: In from the Cold   139

Chapter Thirty-Five: Big Screen   143

Chapter Thirty-Six: Zak   145

Chapter Thirty-Seven: Game Over   149

Chapter Thirty-Eight: A New Challenger   153

Chapter Thirty-Nine: Champion   159

Chapter Forty: The Glory of the Queen   161

This is a 1989 Ford F-150.

To you, the reader of this story, it probably looks like an old truck.

But to me, the main character of this story, it looked like a new truck, because this story is set in 1989.

In 1989, I lived in a little house with my mom and two rabbits. That meant when my mom couldn't find a babysitter, I had to go along with her and her boyfriend when they went out on dates. Her boyfriend was named Craig. The truck belonged to him.

We were all three in Craig's truck.

Craig was driving.
My mom was in the passenger seat.

I was smooshed in the back.

Even though I was not a tall kid (I was the shortest boy in my class), things in the back of Craig's truck were still pretty smooshed.

I could have sat in the front of the truck, in between Craig and my mom. But when I sat there, Craig would rest his bicep on my head when he reached over to put his arm around my mom.

I preferred the smooshing.

I had my Game Boy with me, and I was playing SPY MASTER.

Instead of being smooshed in the back of a truck, I was hiding behind plants, cracking safes, and stealing secret plans. My eyes focused on the screen while my thumbs worked away—Up, Down, Left, Right, A, B. Press the right button at the right time, and everything would be OK.

I felt my mom tap me on the knee. I glanced up at her, hoping I wouldn't have to pause my game.

But she was motioning for me to take off my headphones.

So I paused my game.

"Craig's asking you a question," my mom said.

"I said," Craig said, "can you hear anything with those headphones on?"

"No," I said.

"Oh," said Craig. He turned to my mom. "I can't believe you let him play that thing."

"He loves it," my mom said.

"Great reason," said Craig.

He looked at me in the rearview mirror.

"Enjoy it while you can, kid. I don't think you'll find a job that lets you sit around playing video games all day."

"Video game tester," I said.

When I was a kid, I wanted to be a video game tester. So did a bunch of other kids in my class, even more than wanted to be marine biologists.

"A video game tester!" said Craig. "You're just making stuff up."

"No," I said, "you can look it up. There's this magazine called *Gamer Mag* that Mom won't get me a subscription for"—my mom rolled her eyes—"and a kid named Zak has a monthly column. He's a video game tester, and he's only thirteen! He's cool!"

"Why's he cool?" Craig asked.

"First of all, he has spiky hair."

"Don't start," my mom said.

COOL ZAK

MAC B. KID SPY

MAC CRACKS THE CODE

By **Mac Barnett**

Illustrated by **Mike Lowery**

Orchard Books
New York
An Imprint of Scholastic Inc.

ME AS A

~~KID~~

SPY!

(I wanted spikes, but my mom didn't like how my hair looked with gel in it.)

"Second of all, he's really good at video games. He's probably the best gamer in the world. Third of all, his name has three letters."

"Why is that cool?" Craig said.

"Because he can put his whole name on a game's high score list!" I said. "Most people can only put their initials."

SCORE	POINTS	NAME
1 ST	1 BILLION	ZAK
2 ND	7,335	TML

"Wow," said Craig. But he didn't mean it.

"And *fourth* of all," I said, "he gets to play new video games before they even come out."

"So he's a professional couch potato," said Craig. "Real cool. *Not.*"

In 1989, lots of people were putting "not" at the end of their sentences, and it was always hilarious. Not.

I shook my head. "You should just read his column. *Gamer Mag* is great. They have reviews, sneak previews, cheat codes—"

"Oh good," said Craig. "You're learning how to cheat."

"No, you enter a cheat code on a game to get power-ups and stuff. It's not really cheating. It's allowed."

Craig pulled into a parking space in front of the movie theater.

"Did you turn off your Game Boy?" my mom asked.

"Yes," I said.

She looked at my Game Boy.

"Then why is that light on?"

I turned off my Game Boy. The screen went blank.

Craig checked his watch. "I don't want to miss the previews."

"Hold on," my mom said. She handed me a bag of Corn Nuts and a pack of licorice.

I put the Corn Nuts in my pocket and tucked in my shirt so I could hide the licorice against my belly.

(We never bought snacks in the movie theater because they jacked up the prices.)

She handed Craig a Dr Pepper.

"Where am I supposed to hide this?" he asked. "Can't you put it in your purse?"

"I brought my clutch," my mom said. "I wanted to look nice. This is a date."

"Some date," Craig said. "Corn Nuts and a kiddie movie."

My mom sighed.

"I'll take it." I grabbed the can and stuffed it down my shirt.

"Can we go now?" Craig asked.

We hurried across the parking lot.

"If they find this food, I don't know you guys," Craig said.

"My hero," said my mom.

"They never check," I said. "They don't care."

I could tell Craig was nervous when the usher was tearing our tickets because there was some sweat above his mustache. But the usher didn't care.

"Theater three, on your right," he said, and gave Craig his tickets back.

We passed the snack bar, a claw machine, and a kid playing an arcade game.

I stopped short.

"Ooh, they have an arcade game now!"

When I was a kid, it was my goal to get my name on as many high score lists on as many arcade machines as I could.

"Can I have a quarter?"

"That boy's already playing," my mom said.

"It doesn't matter," I said. "It's a fighting game. If I put in a quarter, I can challenge him. That's arcade rules."

"We're going to miss the previews!" Craig said.

"I can't give you quarters every time we pass a video game," my mom said.

"Please!" I said. "I love fighting games."

"Come on!" Craig dug into his jeans pocket. "Here's a quarter. How 'bout you use it *after* the movie."

"Thanks, Craig," I said.

That was nice of him.

It always bugged me when Craig did nice things. Luckily, he usually ruined it by doing something that wasn't nice in the next ten minutes.

"Now let's go!" Craig said. "We're missing the previews!"

The previews hadn't started yet.

We took our seats. I couldn't stop thinking about the game in the lobby.

"Did you know they're going to come out with a SPY MASTER fighting game?" I asked.

"Oh yeah?" my mom said.

I could tell she wasn't really paying attention.

"Yeah," I said. "There was a sneak preview in *Gamer Mag*."

"Oh," she said.

"They're going to unveil it soon at the Video Game World Championships. Do you guys know what that is?"

I could tell neither of them wanted to hear about the Video Game World Championships. When I was a kid, sometimes the things I cared most about wouldn't interest adults one bit, but I would get so excited I couldn't stop talking. I knew Craig and my mom wished they could have a date without me, and I also wished they could have a date without me, and yet there we were.

Craig sighed.

"It's the first-ever global video game tournament.

Gamers from around the world will flock to New York City to compete on behalf of their countries and prove, once and for all, who's the Champion Supreme of the Arcade Machine. That's how *Gamer Mag* put it. I really wish we subscribed."

My mom sighed.

"Every arcade game has a high score list," I said, "with the names of the best players to ever play that machine. But the Video Game World Championships will have the high score list for the entire *planet*."

"Uh-huh," said Craig.

"I mean, maybe the entire universe," I said. "Because even if there's intelligent life on other planets, that doesn't mean that aliens would have video games. Although if they have advanced technology, I bet they *would* have video games, because—"

The lights dimmed.

"The previews!" Craig said.

The previews started, and I stopped talking, and

we were all glad about that.

There was one about a police dog, and one about a weird uncle, and one about a talking baby.

Craig leaned over to me and whispered, "Hey, buddy, could I get that Dr Pepper?"

"I think it's for all of us," I whispered back.

"It's cool, I'll share."

I took a look at Craig's mustache.

"Hmmm."

I reached down my shirt and gave him the soda.

When Craig opened the can, there was that little spritzing sound, then that metal cracking sound. Craig took a deep swallow and then, so loud the whole theater could hear, said, "Ahhhhhhhh."

The usher came up to our row with a flashlight and said, "Excuse me."

"He brought it!" Craig said.

"Kid," said the usher, "would you come with me?"

My mom stood up. "This is ridiculous. If you didn't jack up your prices—"

"I don't care about that," said the usher. "It's just . . . there's a phone call for this kid."

Craig was dumbfounded.

"Who would call him?" Craig asked.

I knew who.

It was the Queen of England.

The usher pointed to a pay phone in the lobby.

"It wouldn't stop ringing, so I picked it up," he said. "It's a lady with an accent. I think maybe she's Australian?"

"She's English," I said.

"Well, she's not very friendly," said the usher.

"She takes some getting used to." I went over to the phone and picked up the receiver.

"Hello?" I said.

"Hullo!" she said. "May I speak to Mac?"

"Speaking," I said.

"Mac," said the Queen of England. "Wherever are you? And who was that who answered the phone? Your butler? Because if it was, I recommend you hire a better butler."

"It wasn't my butler," I said. "It was a teenager. I'm at a movie theater at the mall."

"Mac, I need you to leave the movie theater immediately and come to England."

"But the movie just started," I said.

"Which film are you seeing?" the Queen of England asked.

"*Honey, I Shrunk the Kids.*"

"Honey, I what the what?"

"*Honey, I Shrunk the Kids.*"

"Mac," said the Queen, "although I have not watched the film, I believe I can tell you what happens. Some kids are shrunk. And unless I am very much mistaken, in the end, the kids will be unshrunk and returned to their normal sizes."

"Well, don't give it away," I said.

"Mac," said the Queen of England, "would you rather return to that movie theater or come to England for a spy mission?"

I turned and looked at theater three. Behind those doors was a man with his arm around my mom and a warm soda that had touched a mustache.

The Queen didn't wait for me to answer.

"A car will arrive for you in five minutes. Good-bye."

She hung up.

I looked over at the arcade game.

I pulled Craig's quarter out of my pocket.

The phone rang, and I picked it up.

It was the Queen of England

"Hello?" I said.

"Hullo," said the Queen of England. "May I speak to Mac?"

"Speaking," I said.

"There's no time for games. Put that quarter away. Good-bye."

CHAPTER

3

KNIGHT OF OLD

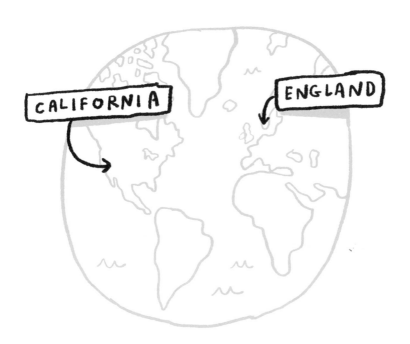

And that's how it happens. One moment you are about to enjoy a movie about shrinking some kids, and the next moment you are in a car that takes you to a plane that takes you to another car that takes you to a palace in England.

You don't really get much say about where you go or what you do when you are a spy. But then again, you don't really get much say about where you go or what you do when you are a kid.

The Queen of England was sitting on a throne, petting a very long dog.

"Finally!" she said.

"It takes a long time to get here from California," I said.

"I suppose that is a good excuse," said the Queen. "However, I despise excuses, even good ones. Simply apologize, and we will move on."

"I'm sorry." I bowed when I said it, to score extra points with the Queen.

"That was a good apology," said the Queen, "but a terrible bow. Don't you agree, Francine?"

Francine let out a yip.

"Mac," said the Queen, "I would like you to meet Francine. Do you know what kind of dog Francine is?"

"A corgi?" I said.

(The Queen of England loved corgis.)

"Wrong!" said the Queen. "Francine is a dorgi."

"A dorgi?" I said.

"A dorgi," said the Queen of England. "Part dachshund, part corgi. Combine the two dogs, and you get Francine. Combine the two words, and you get 'dorgi.' It is a portmanteau."

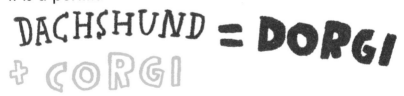

"Neat!" I said.

"Do you know what a portmanteau is?"

"Nope!" I said.

"It is a suitcase made of two compartments. A portmanteau is also a word made with two words. Like smog: 'smoke' and 'fog.' Or chortle: 'chuckle' and 'snort.'"

"Or spork!" I said.

"Spork?" said the Queen of England.

"Yeah, a spork is part spoon, part fork. It's a plastic thingie they give you at fast-food restaurants."

"Mac, I found everything you just said to be absolutely disgusting."

"OK," I said.

"In any case, dorgis are wonderful dogs. And I should know. I invented them!"

"You invented them?"

"Yes! You can look it up! The dorgi was my idea!"

"How do you invent a dog?" I asked.

"When I was a young girl," said the Queen, "one of my corgis sneaked out and paid a visit to one of my sister's dachshunds, and nine weeks later—hullo!—we had a litter of little dorgis."

"Sounds like it was your corgi's idea," I said.

The Queen of England frowned.

But Francine seemed to think it was funny.

"In any case," said the Queen, "I did not fly you all the way out to London to sit and gab about dorgis. I have a mission for you. It is a matter of great international importance."

"Hold it there," I said.

"*Excuse* me?" said the Queen.

"I mean, you may please hold it right there, Your Majesty, because I think I already know what the mission is."

"Do you?"

"Yes," I said. "You are sending me to the Video Game World Championships in New York City."

The Queen of England smiled. "Continue."

"As I'm sure I don't need to tell you, this week gamers from around the world will flock to New York City to prove, once and for all, who's the Champion Supreme of the Arcade Machine."

The Queen raised her eyebrows.

"This year, players will have to prove themselves on SPY MASTER: BATTLE EDITION, a brand-new video game nobody in the world has played. Now, who is great at SPY MASTER? Me! And who else is great at SPY MASTER? The KGB Man!"

The KGB Man was a spy from the Soviet Union. In the 1980s, the Soviet Union was a country. Today it doesn't exist.

But the Soviet Union was Britain's archenemy.

And the KGB Man was my archenemy.

The main reason he was my archenemy was that, one time, he had stolen my pants.

But another big reason he was my archenemy was that, another time, he had stolen my Game Boy.

Eventually, he gave my Game Boy back, but only after he'd beaten my high score on SPY MASTER. And I still hadn't been able to reclaim the number-one slot.

(And he still hadn't given me back my jeans.)

"I bet the Soviet Union will send the KGB Man to the championships," I said. "And if he wins, he will put the KGB's initials atop the high score list of the entire world!

22

The high score list of the entire universe, if aliens don't have video games, which they probably do! And that is why you are sending me to compete in the tourney on your behalf, like a knight of old!"

I lowered myself to one knee.

"Your Majesty," I said, "I am at your service."

The Queen of England frowned.

I could tell she was frowning, even though I was looking at the floor.

"What are you doing?" she asked.

"Kneeling," I said. "Like a knight of old."

"Well stand up," said the Queen. "This mission has nothing to do with the Video Game World Championships."

"It doesn't?"

"No," said the Queen. "The Americans are handling that."

"I'm American," I said.

"Yes," said the Queen. "But you work for me. And I, thank goodness, am *not* American."

"Hey!" I said.

"In any case," said the Queen of England, "the President of the United States of America assures me that he has the Video Game World Championships under control. He is sending someone named, let me see here . . ." She pulled an envelope marked TOP SECRET out of her purse and studied its contents. "Zak."

"Oh," I said.

"There's a photo of him here. Would you like to see?"

"I know what he looks like. I read his column in *Gamer Mag*."

"His hair is quite spiky, like a porcupine's back."

"Yeah," I said. "I want to do my hair like that, but my mom won't let me."

"I agree with her," said the Queen. "Very few people are capable of wearing a hairstyle like that without looking ridiculous. I very much doubt you are one of them. Leave the spikes and the video games to Zak. It's time to talk about spying."

CHAPTER

4

TRADECRAFT

"We have been aware for some time of an enemy spy operating on our shores. He has been skulking around London, making dead drops, exchanging pass-phrases with shady characters. I must say, his trade-craft has been quite obvious."

"Yes," I said. "I see."

"Mac." The Queen gave me a stern glance. "Do you know what tradecraft means?"

"No," I said. "Is it a portmanteau?"

"No," said the Queen. "It is just a compound word. In a portmanteau the words are smooshed together more."

"OK," I said.

The Queen continued. "How about dead drops?"

"A portmanteau."

"No," said the Queen. "Dead drop is two separate words. Do you know what a passphrase is?"

"Can I see it written down?"

"Mac, we are no longer talking about portmanteau words. We are talking about spying. Tradecraft refers to the things spies do. Such as sneaking. Such as eavesdropping. Such as dead drops."

"OK," I said.

"A dead drop is when a spy leaves something for another spy in a secret location, taped beneath a bench in the park, for instance. In this case, the spy was hiding secret messages in the light of a phone booth in Blackheath."

"Neat!" I said.

"Indeed," said the Queen. "Now. A live drop is when two spies meet in person. And since they probably will not know each other, they establish their identities by using passphrases—a bunch of secret passwords that sound to anyone nearby like a normal conversation. For instance, you might approach me at a bus stop and say, 'Mozart is my favorite composer.' And then I would say, 'Yes, I quite adore his Horn Concerto No. 4 in E-flat major.' And then you would say, 'Bah! I prefer woodwinds, and so enjoy his Oboe Concerto in C major.' And now we would each know the other was a spy, although to anyone listening it would sound like we were just two strangers having a normal conversation."

"That doesn't sound normal," I said. "I don't think that's what people talk about when they meet each other."

"No?" said the Queen. "Then what do you think they talk about?"

I shrugged. "I don't know. I don't really meet that many people."

"Nor do I," said the Queen. "Perhaps that is why you and I get on so well."

"We do?" I said.

"Moving on!" said the Queen. "Last night, we raided the spy's apartment and arrested him. A thorough search of his apartment revealed almost nothing of interest: a paperback novel, a drab suit, a pair of black socks, and a pair of white pants."

I nodded seriously. "Underwear," I said.

"Excuse me?" said the Queen.

"What you call pants, we call underwear."

"Yes, I know," said the Queen.

"OK," I said.

"Now," said the Queen, "there was a label sewn into the pants. But instead of a label that said Marks & Spencer—do you have Marks & Spencer in America?"

"No," I said.

"Who makes your underwear?"

"That's personal!" I said.

"I mean who makes *Americans'* underwear," said the Queen of England. "What is an American brand of underwear?"

"Oh! Um. Underoos."

"Underoos?"

"They're underwear with cartoon characters on them. Hey! I think it's a portmanteau word!"

"Of what?"

"Underwear and . . . kangaroos?"

The Queen gave me a disapproving look. "Seems ridiculous."

"I never said I wear Underoos!" I said.

(But I did wear them.)

"Moving on!" said the Queen. "Instead of a label that said, for instance"—the Queen rolled her eyes—"Underoos, this label said nothing at all."

"Hmmm," I said. "That's sort of interesting."

"Until we looked at it under an ultraviolet light. When we discovered a writing in secret ink."

"Wow!" I said. "That's very interesting!"

"Yes!" said the Queen.

"What did the writing say?"

"It said . . ." The Queen leaned forward. "DRUBBA-LUBBA."

"DRUBBALUBBA?"

"Yes, I think I have that right." She reached into her purse and removed a slip of paper and some reading glasses. "Yes! Yes. DRUBBALUBBA."

"Oh," I said. "What does that mean?"

"I haven't the faintest idea," said the Queen. "It's a secret code. And it seems to be unbreakable. Ever since we discovered the message, we've been throwing everything we have into cracking it. A team of cryptologists, who are people who study codes, and not people who study graves, which would not be useful in this context. A roomful of supercomputers. An army of maths teachers from Oxbridge, which is a portmanteau of two very fancy schools called Oxford and Cambridge, and not a bridge for oxen, which would not be useful in any context, unless I suppose you were an ox farmer who lived near a river."

"I'm sorry," I said, "'maths teachers'?"

"Yes," said the Queen of England. "What do you call them in America?"

"We just call them math teachers."

"Well," said the Queen, "that sounds ridiculous."

"Hmmm," I said.

"Mac," said the Queen, "here is your mission: I need you to sit alone in a room in this palace with a pencil and see if you can crack this code."

CHAPTER

6

A RECKLESS SPY

"That's it?" I said.

"That's it," said the Queen.

"But normally my missions involve chases and blow-ing stuff up."

"Yes." The Queen grimaced. "I must talk to you about that. On your last mission, a submarine explod-ed right here, on the River Thames."

"Yeah!" I said.

"Mac," said the Queen, "it is one thing to go about wrecking things in another country, such as France. It is quite another to cause havoc here. That is why I am taking you out of the field and placing you behind a desk."

"What!"

"You are reckless. You are dangerous. You are sloppy. Although I am happy to see that you're tucking in your shirt these days."

"Oh!" I said. "This is just so I could sneak food into the movie. My mom never buys candy at the theater."

"Your mother is a smart woman," said the Queen. "The prices are outrageous."

"But you're rich!" I said.

"Indeed I am," said the Queen. "And I would not be nearly so rich if I purchased licorice at the theater."

"Actually, wait a second!" I reached down the front

of my shirt and pulled out the box of Red Vines. "I forgot this was still in here. Want one?"

"Yes," said the Queen.

I handed her a licorice stick. She chewed on the end.

"Remember: your mission is to figure out the meaning of DRUBBALUBBA. Nothing more, and nothing less."

"But this is the most boring mission of all time!" I said.

The Queen nodded. "That is the point."

CHEW
CHEW

CHAPTER

7

BETWEEN YOU AND ME

WINK

(Don't worry though. If this actually were a boring mission, I wouldn't have written a book about it.)

CHAPTER

8

PAPERWORK

I sat alone in a room with a desk, a pencil, and a
blank sheet of paper.

At the top of the piece of paper I wrote, as neatly
as I could,

It wasn't very neat.

I had terrible handwriting.

"DRUBBALUBBA," I said. "DRUBBA . . . LUBBA."

I erased it and tried to write it again neater.

What did it mean!

I decided to start by seeing if the letters were all
scrambled up.

Maybe it was like Boggle! I played Boggle every Thursday night with my mom and Craig. Craig *loved* Boggle, probably because he usually beat me.

I pretended like Craig was sitting across the table from me and rearranged DRUBBALUBBA into as many combinations as I could think of.

"Aha!" I said to myself. "That's it! A bald guy, whose name is Bub, is going to . . . rub . . . something! I cracked it! Now I can go home!"

"Mac," I replied to myself, "the Queen of England is never going to buy that."

I wasn't very good at Boggle.

For a second, I wished Craig would knock on the door, come into the room, solve the puzzle, and then immediately leave again, preferably without saying anything to me.

Then I shook my head and knocked that wish out of my brain.

I would solve this puzzle *myself*.

I stared at the piece of paper on my desk.

I put down my pencil.

I sighed.

I gnawed on a piece of licorice and stared out the window.

It had gotten dark.

The sky was black.

The trees were black.

The ground was black.

What was I doing? I was getting nowhere, cooped up here in a cozy lamplit room.

One day, if video game testing didn't work out, I might spend my days at a desk staring at a white piece of paper.

But for now, I was a kid.

And I was a spy.

And if I was going to crack this code, I belonged out there, in the night.

I went over to the window and lifted the sash.
It slid open. Cold air blew into the room.
I poked my head outside.

Luckily, I was on the first floor, so there wasn't much
of a drop.

I climbed up and straddled the windowsill. Half of
my body was inside, and half of my body was out.

"Here we go," I said.

If I dropped over to the other side, there was no turning back. The Queen would be furious. I could not return until I had cracked that code.

"One," I said.

"Two," I said.

There was a knock on the door.

KNOCK
KNOCK

It was the Queen of England.

"Hullo?" she said.

"Hello," I called back into the room.

"Just wanted to check in on how things are going," said the Queen.

"Really well," I said.

"Wonderful," said the Queen. "Also, I wanted to get another stick of licorice from you."

"Oh," I said. "Um."

I saw the door's handle turn.

"I'll just come in and get it."

I tipped over and dropped onto the wet grass.

"Mac?"

I scrambled to my feet and ran across the lawn.

"Mac!"

The Queen appeared in the window I had just es-caped from.

"MAC!" she cried. "Guards! Guards! Mac has gone rogue!"

Sirens blared.

Bright lights swept across the ground.

Guards poured out of the palace.

I zigzagged across the lawn, avoiding the search-
lights' paths.

"Over here!" someone said nearby.

"Over there!" someone said, also nearby.

"Here!"

"There!"

"Here!"

There were lots of guards, and they were all nearby.

I ducked behind a rosebush and tried to make myself very small, which was not too hard, because I was very small for my grade. Craig always told my mom that I would grow more if she stopped letting me eat cinnamon graham crackers all the time and fed me more steak.

Crouching beneath that rosebush outside Buckingham Palace, I was glad I ate all those cinnamon graham crackers. "Take that, Craig" is something I would have said out loud, if I wasn't hiding from a bunch of guards.

There was a fence a few yards away.

If I just waited for the right moment, I could climb that fence and escape into the city.

Until then, I would stay in my hiding place, where nobody could see me.

BARK!
BARK!

Just then, furious barking filled the air.

Dogs.

Nobody could see me, but dogs could sure smell me.

I curled up in a little ball and tried to rub dirt all over myself to cover up my smell.

But it was no use.

A shadow bounded across the lawn.

It stopped beside my rosebush, growling, snapping, and baring its teeth.

I peered out at the dog and trembled.

It licked its chops.

Wait—

I knew that tongue.

I knew that dog.

I whispered, "Hello, Freddie."

CHAPTER

11

GUARD DOG

Freddie was the smallest of the Queen's corgis. The Queen often loaned him to me when I went on my spy missions, but when I was done I had to give him back. He was probably my best friend.

Freddie stopped growling. He stood next to my rosebush and yapped happily.

I think I was Freddie's best friend too.

"Be quiet, Freddie," I whispered. "Please."

Freddie kept yapping.

"Freddie, go away."

He did not go away.

"Freddie, you'll alert the guards."

Freddie didn't care.

"I'm a rogue agent now, Freddie. You can't come with me. I act alone."

Freddie wagged his tail.

Pleading with Freddie wasn't working.

I was going to have to do something I'd seen in a bunch of dog movies, at the part when the kid needs the dog to go away, for the dog's own good.

This was going to be unpleasant.

I made a serious face and began my big speech.

"Freddie, you're a bad dog."

Freddie looked confused.

"You're a really bad dog, and I don't like you anymore. We're not friends, Freddie. Go live your life. I never want to see you again! Go! Go away!"

Freddie ducked under the rosebush and started licking my face.

"Aw man," I said.

"Oi!" said one of the guards. "Someone should check over there, in the rose garden."

I scratched Freddie behind his ears.

"OK," I said. "Let's go."

I tucked Freddie down the front of my shirt like a box of licorice, slipped out from the cover of the Queen's garden, and climbed the fence.

Freddie and I disappeared into the city.

CHAPTER

12

DEAD DROP

A heath is a big, wild area full of plants and animals, and this heath is right in the middle of London. Blackheath is mostly green, so it's kind of a strange name.

But in 1348, three hundred years after Blackheath was named, a terrible plague called the black death swept through London. Almost half the city died. And many of them were buried in the ground below Blackheath. So it turned out to be a good name.

When I stood in Blackheath in 1989, a rogue spy alone on a cold night, the grass did not look green. The heath was a tangle of shadows and fog. So Blackheath felt like a *very* good name.

I had a hunch:

The Queen of England said the captured spy had been exchanging messages with another spy by leaving them in a phone booth in Blackheath.

Well: If the spy was sitting in a cell now, that meant that he couldn't go around picking up dead drops.

And *that* meant there might be a message waiting for him in a phone booth.

And if I found that message, it might just give me a clue that would help me break the code.

DRUBBALUBBA!

I snuggled Freddie to my chest to stay warm and surveyed the area.

A church bell rang one from a tall spire.

A twisted tree trunk made a sinister silhouette.

A big fox padded past on some secret business.

Freddie got a whiff of the fox and tried to scramble out of my shirt.

"Stop it, Freddie," I said. "You're ruining the mood."

Across the heath, a friendly yellow light shone in a red phone booth.

Aha!

I ran across the heath, above the seven-hundred-year-old bones buried below the grass, and entered the booth.

It was warm inside, and there was a bright bulb up in the ceiling.

The Queen said that the spies had hidden their messages in the phone booth's light!

I reached up and hoped I would find what I was looking for.

I wasn't tall enough to reach the light.

Not even close.

"Aw man," I said.

I tried jumping, but I wasn't a great jumper, especially with a dog in my shirt.

I set Freddie on the ground and tried climbing up on the phone, but I wasn't a great climber, even without a dog in my shirt.

I even tried to shimmy up the booth, but I was afraid I was going to break the glass.

"I need a boost, Freddie."

Freddie looked up at me.

"Not from you, Freddie. Something strong, like a rock."

Freddie's tongue lolled.

"Yes, a rock!" I said.

I exited the booth and searched for the right rock.

Some rocks were big enough but too heavy.

Some rocks I could carry but were too small to work.

For a wilderness, this place sure was short on rocks.

"How hard is it to find a good rock on this blasted heath?" I said, to Freddie I guess.

Finally, by a murky pond, I came across a rock that looked about right.

I hauled it back to the booth and pushed it inside.

I stood on the rock.

I reached up to the lamp and swiped my hand above it, feeling for anything suspicious.

"Come on," I said. "Come on!"

My fingers brushed against something strange.

CHAPTER

13

CRYPTIC MESSAGE

TOP SECRET

It was a piece of paper, folded up tightly.

I eagerly unwrapped it.

A secret message!

ETEM EM NI
KOOTY UDYEATS
FIND THE EMPEROR
OF FRANCE, AND GO
UP TO THE BATHROOM
ON THE THIRD FLOOR
— AT 3:00 P.M.
BRING THE
CODE.

I stared at it.

The first sentence was encrypted.

The second sentence contained instructions.

And the third sentence referred to a code.

DRUBBALUBBA.

This was a big break.

I was getting much further than I ever could behind a desk.

"Take that, Your Majesty," I whispered to the night.

Just then the phone rang.

CHAPTER

19

ROGUE AGENT

I didn't want to pick it up.

But I did.

It was the Queen of England.

"Hello?" I said.

"Hullo," said the Queen. "May I speak to Mac?"

"Speaking," I said.

"Mac," said the Queen. "Give up this nonsense immediately. You are to return to Buckingham Palace, where you will be assigned some even more menial task as a punishment."

"That sounds awful," I said.

"It is an order!" said the Queen.

"You can't give me orders, Your Majesty," I said. "I'm a rogue agent."

I hung up the phone.

It started ringing again.

I left the phone booth and walked out onto the heath.

For a long time, I could hear the phone ringing behind me.

CHAPTER
15

EMPEROR OF FRANCE

I stood in the glow of a streetlamp and took another look at the message.

I didn't know where to find the Emperor of France.
But I knew someone who would.
So I went to France.

CHAPTER 16

PASSPHRASE

Early the next morning, I sat at a quiet sidewalk café, eating a pastry, reading a copy of *Gamer Mag*.

At the table next to mine, a man with a sad face drank a coffee.

It was the President of France.

"Bonjour," I said.

"Hello," he said.

"Mozart is my favorite composer," I said.

The President of France looked confused.

"That's nice," he said.

I frowned.

"*Mozart* is my favorite *composer*," I said.

"I heard you," said the President of France. "I am very happy for you."

"That's not what you're supposed to say," I said. "Didn't you get my message?"

"Yes." The President of France pulled out a piece of paper. "It said to meet you here at 6:00 a.m. And so here I am. Why? I do not know."

"There was a second page," I said. "With pass-phrases. You're supposed to say 'Yes, I quite adore his Horn Concerto No. 4 in E-flat major.'"

"But why?" said the President of France. "I do not like the horns. I prefer woodwinds."

"That's *my* line!" I dropped my fork, and it clattered on my plate. This was ridiculous.

"This is ridiculous," said the President of France. "Why would we say these things?"

"It's so we know who the other guy is," I said, "and so we can trust each other."

"But we already know each other," said the President of France.

"Ah," I said.

He had a point. The President of France and I had met on my very first mission. We were old friends.

"And I do not trust you," he said.

"Ah," I said.

"And so," said the President of France, "I would like you to tell me what the Queen of England wants, and then leave this country as soon as possible."

"I don't work for the Queen anymore. I went rogue." I took a bite of my croissant. "I answer to nobody but myself. Listen: I want you to take me to the Emperor of France."

The President of France chuckled sadly.

"But there is no Emperor of France," he said.

CHAPTER

17

RED HERRING

"There isn't?" I asked.

"No," said the President of France. "France does not have an emperor."

"It doesn't?" I asked.

"No. France has a president. Me."

"Right," I said, "but I thought maybe above you—"

The President of France grimaced. "There is nobody in France above me," he said. "I answer to nobody but myself."

"Hmmm," I said.

"There has not been an Emperor of France for more than one hundred years. France has had only three emperors, and they all had the same name: Napoleon."

"Napoleon?"

"Yes. Napoleon I, Napoleon II, and Napoleon III."

1 2 3

"A trilogy!" I said. "Which one is the best?"

The President of France shrugged. "I suppose people prefer the first one."

I nodded. "That's usually how it is."

I chewed my breakfast and had a think.

"It's just . . ."

I took out the secret message from the phone booth.

"An enemy spy left this message for another enemy spy, and I'm trying to figure it out."

The President of France studied the note.

"Well," he said, "there is only one emperor left in the world. The Emperor of Japan. Perhaps you should go talk to him."

I pointed to the paper. "But it says the Emperor of *France*."

"Yes, but this might be a red herring," said the President.

"Right," I said.

We stared at each other.

"What is a red herring?" I asked.

"It is a lie made to look like a clue. A finger that points in the wrong direction. A sign you are meant to ignore."

"OK," I said.

"Besides," said the President of France, "the secret code at the top is pretty clear."

"Right," I said.

We stared at each other again.

"What does it say?" I asked.

"The letters are all scrambled," said the President.

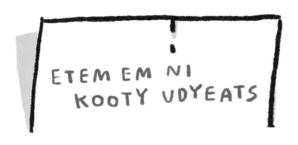

"What does it say?" I asked.

"The letters are all scrambled," said the President.

"What does it say!" I asked again.

75

CHAPTER

18

BOGGLED

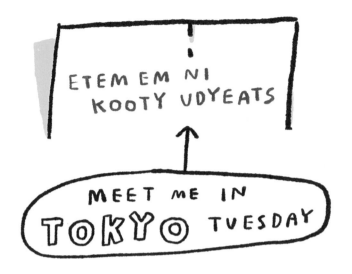

"It says MEET ME IN TOKYO TUESDAY," said the President of France.

"Wow!" I said. "You must be really great at Boggle!"

The President of France nodded sadly. "I am excellent at Boggle."

"I wish you'd come over to my house some Thursday and whoop this guy I know."

"Craig?" said the President.

"Yeah," I said.

"I remember." He sipped his coffee. "Craig is your stepfather, yes?"

"No," I said quickly. "He's just dating my mom."

"Still," said the President, "it sounds serious."

"OK," I said. "Anyway. Hey, since you're pretty great at codes, maybe you can tell me this. What does DRUBBALUBBA mean?"

"DRUBBALUBBA?"

He handed me a pen and a napkin.
"Write it down," he said.
I did.

"Hmmm," said the President. "A Bald Bub Rub?"

"OK," I said. "Thanks for trying."
I put the napkin in my pocket.
"I am sorry I could not help more."
"You helped plenty," I said. "That was great. 'MEET ME IN TOKYO TUESDAY.'"
I started.
"But tomorrow is Tuesday!" I said.
"It is," said the President. "You'd better get to Japan."

I stood up.
"I will!" I said.

CHAPTER

19

A FAVOR

I stayed standing there.

"Hey," I said. "Um. Do you think you could buy me a plane ticket? I'm sure the Queen of England will pay you back when this is all over."

I never saw him look so sad.

"Yes," he said.

CHAPTER

20

PEACE EVERYWHERE

日本

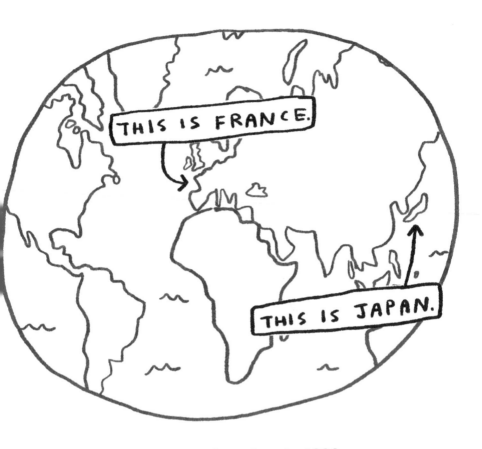

In France, this story takes place in 1989.

That is because France uses the Gregorian calendar.

The Gregorian calendar was introduced by a pope whose name was Gregory.

(Good name.)

It is the most commonly used calendar in the world.

But it's not the only calendar. There are lots.

Japan has its own calendar. It groups years into eras.

A new era begins each time a new emperor rises to the throne.

So this story also takes place in Heisei 1—the first year of the Heisei era.

And I am writing this story in Heisei 30—the last year of the Heisei era.

Heisei means "peace everywhere," and from the time this story takes place to the time this story was written, Japan has not been at war.

(Good name.)

Since it was Heisei 1, that meant there was a new Emperor of Japan.

And this is where he lived:

The Imperial Palace is in the middle of Tokyo's tall buildings.

It is surrounded by a moat and tucked away inside a forest.

Goshawks and butterflies fly in the air.

Prawns and carp flit down in the moats.

Raccoon dogs, which are neither raccoons nor dogs, climb in the trees.

The small Japanese mole burrows underground.

And on Tuesday morning, a rogue spy walked across the Seimon Ishibashi bridge.

The Seimon Ishibashi bridge is a stone bridge that leads up to the main gate of the Emperor's palace. Its name translates to "Main Gate Stone Bridge."

(Good name.)

(Although a lot of people call it the Eyeglass Bridge, and as you can see, that's a good name too.)

I found the Emperor of Japan by a stream in the gardens, feeding some fish.

"Ah, the rogue agent. The President of France told me to expect you."

He looked at me. "I thought you'd be taller."

I nodded. "Everybody says that."

He handed me a basket. "Would you like to feed them?"

I looked inside. "What is this stuff?"

"Lettuce and garlic," he said. "It's good for them."

I tossed some lettuce leaves and garlic cloves into the stream.

(On the sly, I slipped some lettuce to Freddie too.)

The hungry fish splashed and opened their eager mouths.

"I love fish," said the Emperor of Japan. "Do you love fish?"

"I'm allergic to cod," I said.

"Not to eat!" said the Emperor. "To think about. Do you love thinking about fish?"

"Oh," I said. "Sure . . ."

"What is your favorite fish?" asked the Emperor of Japan.

"Um," I said. "Well. Definitely not cod."

"Mine is the goby," said the Emperor.

"Cool," I said.

We looked at each other.

"What is a goby?"

The Emperor's eyes lit up. "The goby is a fish with a big head and a body that tapers down to a small tail. Now, and this is very important, you can always tell a goby by the specific arrangement of their sensory papillae—"

"Hmmm," I said.

"You know," he said, "I do not mean to boast, but in addition to being the Emperor of Japan, I am also one of the world's top experts on gobies."

(That's true. You can look it up.)

"Wait here," said the Emperor. "I will fetch my article, 'Some Morphological Characters Considered to Be Important in Gobiid Phylogeny.' I think you will find it very interesting."

"Hmmm," I said.

He turned and started walking away.

"Your Majesty," I said, "I'm sorry, but I did not come here to talk to you about gobies."

"Of course not," he said. "Sometimes I get carried away. If I weren't an emperor, I should have liked to have been a marine biologist. Why did you come here?"

"I came here because I think a spy will try to make a live drop at your palace in just a few hours."

"Oh!" said the Emperor of Japan. "Well that is very interesting too!"

CHAPTER

21

BATHROOM TALK

"Here is the deal," I said. "At three o'clock this afternoon, a spy will arrive here, at your palace. He wants to get a secret code from another spy. But what he doesn't know is that instead of meeting the man he's expecting, he'll come face-to-face with me."

If I pretended to be the spy who was in jail, I could meet up with the other spy. After all, he didn't know who he'd be meeting. It was the perfect way to intercept the code!

"Oh, wow," said the Emperor of Japan.

"I have some questions for that spy," I said. "Well, mainly I have one question. What does DRUBBALUBBA mean?"

"DRUBBALUBBA?"

I showed him the secret code.

The Emperor of Japan thought it over.

"Maybe it is a cipher," he said. "In a cipher, each of the letters stands in for another letter. So a D could be an A. Or a B."

"Or a C!" I said.

"Exactly."

"But then," I said, "DRUBBALUBBA could mean almost anything."

"Yes."

"Well that's not very helpful."

"No," said the Emperor of Japan. "Sorry."

"In that case"—I checked my watch—"in about three hours, may I use your bathroom?"

The Emperor of Japan tossed some lettuce to his fish.

"That is an odd question," he said.

"Particularly," I said, "may I use the bathroom on the third floor of your palace?"

"That is an even odder question," said the Emperor of Japan. "My palace is only two stories tall."

"What?" I said.

"Look." He pointed to the building behind him.

(You can look too. Just flip back to page 84.)

"But," I said. "But."

I pulled out the message I'd found in the phone booth.

The Emperor of Japan studied it.

"But this says 'Find the Emperor of France.' I am the Emperor of Japan."

"Probably a red herring," I said. "Do you know what that is?"

"Yes, a fake clue," said the Emperor of Japan. "Of course, a herring is also a kind of fish, of the family *Clupeidae*, although they are not red but silver—"

This guy sure liked fish.

"Sorry," I said, "if we could just stay focused. Look here at the top—this unscrambles to 'MEET ME IN TOKYO TUESDAY.'"

"Yes," said the Emperor of Japan. He smiled. "But it might also unscramble to something else."

Can *you* solve it?

The answer is on page 93!

(Just keep reading.)

CHAPTER

22

ANAGRAMS

"'MEET ME IN *KYOTO* TUESDAY.'"

"Kyoto?" I said. "What's that?"

"It's a city," said the Emperor. "It used to be the capital of Japan."

"Really?" I said.

"Yes, for about a thousand years," said the Emperor of Japan. "That is how it got its nickname: 'The Thousand-Year Capital.'"

"Good nickname," I said.

The Emperor of Japan smiled.

"Wow," I said, "what are the chances? Kyoto and Tokyo share all the same letters!"

"Well," said the Emperor, "not in Japanese."

"Still, it's pretty wild that they do in English, right?"

"Eh," he said. "I guess."

We stared at the fish for a while.

"Anyway," said the Emperor of Japan, "if we go to Kyoto, I can take you to the Emperor of France."

I frowned. "You can?"

"Mac," he said, "have you ever heard of a company called Nintendo?"

CHAPTER
23

HAD I EVER HEARD OF A COMPANY CALLED NINTENDO?

"Yes," I said.

"I will tell you a story."

The Emperor's voice came through a big headset I had over my ears. Otherwise I would not have been able to hear him. We were in a helicopter, flying to Kyoto, and it was noisy.

"In Meiji 22—"

"When's that?" I asked.

"1889."

"Oh boy," I said.

"*In Meiji 22*," said the Emperor of Japan, "a man named Fusajiro Yamauchi started Nintendo."

"You may please hold it right there, Your Majesty," I said. "I don't think they had video games one hundred years ago."

"Nintendo didn't always make video games," said the Emperor of Japan. "In 1889, Nintendo made playing cards.

"But in the 1950s, people weren't buying enough playing cards. So Nintendo became a taxi company,

which failed, and then a TV network,

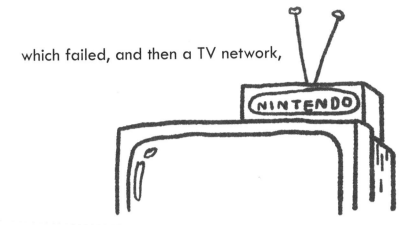

which also failed.

They even sold instant rice.

But it wasn't great rice. So that failed too.

Finally, Nintendo started making toys."

"Good call," I said.

"There was the Nintendo Ultra Hand, which is great for reaching things if you're short."

"Hmmm," I said.

"The Nintendo Ultra Machine, which pitched base-balls, which is great if you don't have anyone to throw a ball around with."

"Hmmm," I said.

"And in 1981," said the Emperor of Japan, "Nintendo made an arcade game called DONKEY KONG."

"Now we're talking!" I said.

"And they've focused on video games ever since. The Game Boy, the Famicom."

"Famicom?"

"In America it's called the NES. Famicom stands for 'family computer.'"

FAMICOM

"A portmanteau word!" I said.

"OK . . ." said the Emperor.

I had spent a lot of quarters on arcade games.

And I had spent a lot of hours playing the NES.

And I had spent even more hours playing my Game Boy.

But I had no idea why the Emperor of Japan was telling me all this.

"Why are you telling me all this?" I asked.

Our helicopter touched down on a cobblestone street.

Its blades stopped whirring.

"Because," said the Emperor of Japan, "back when Nintendo made playing cards, their most famous deck came in a box with a portrait of the Emperor of France."

"You mean—"

"Come," he said. "Let's look across the street."

He led me up to a three-story building.

There was a green sign with gold letters on the wall near the door.

There were two gold circles on the sign. The one on the right said "GOOD FORTUNE" in Japanese. The other one said:

"I have taken you to the Emperor of France, here in Kyoto."

"It wasn't a red herring!" I said.

"You know," said the Emperor, "I've always felt that term was unfair to herring, which are remarkable fish. They travel in schools of up to—"

"Your Majesty," I said, "I think I should get going."

"Of course," said the Emperor of Japan. "I wish I could help you, but I am already late for a meeting of the Ichthyological Society of Japan." He paused. "Do you know what that is?"

"Something to do with fish?" I said.

"Yes!" He hopped into the helicopter and shouted over the noise of the blades. "Good luck with your mission!"

Then he took off.

It was just me and Freddie.

And we were about to infiltrate Nintendo head-quarters.

Technically, Nintendo's main headquarters was across town.

Cool building! It sort of looks like it's made out of a bunch of Game Boys!

Anyway, Freddie and I were about to infiltrate Nintendo's *original* headquarters.

I had to get up to the third floor.

And I had a plan.

CHAPTER

27

DISGUISE

A woman sat behind a desk in a dim lobby. There were faded posters for arcade games all over the walls. "Excuse me," said the woman. "This building is not open to tourists."

I walked up to her desk.

"I am not a tourist," I said. "I'm Mac."

"Matt?" said the woman.

"Mac," I said.

She frowned. "I don't know who you are. Unauthorized personnel must—"

While she was talking, I stuck my hand in front of Freddie's face.

Freddie only had one trick.

It wasn't even really a trick.

He licked stuff.

Freddie game my hand a big lick. The woman picked up a phone and started dialing security.

I ran my wet hand through my hair to give myself spikes.

"My name is Mac," I said. "And I'm a video game tester."

CHAPTER

28

SPY MASTER:
BATTLE EDITION

"Oh!" The woman smiled. "Please come with me. Our testing center is up on the third floor."

The third floor!

"Nice work, Freddie!" I whispered. Then I had him lick my hand again and I gave him spikes too.

I hurried after the woman.

We climbed up a dark staircase and turned a corner into a dusty hall.

She opened a door to a bright white room with an arcade machine inside.

"No way," I said. "No," I said, "way."

The woman smiled and nodded. "Yes."

It was SPY MASTER: BATTLE EDITION.

"Tomorrow, SPY MASTER: BATTLE EDITION will make its debut at the Video Game World Championships in New York City. We expect it to be the greatest fighting game ever made. BLUE SPY and RED SPY battle it out in the Secret Headquarters Building. And you, Mac, will be the first kid in the world to play it."

"Wow."

I approached the machine.

The screen flashed INSERT COIN.

She handed me a bag full of Japanese money.

"Your assignment today is very important. We need you to lose every fight."

"What?"

"Yes. There are still some bugs in the software. When a character does his finishing moves, sometimes

112

the game freezes. Sometimes the screen turns green. And sometimes the finishing move deals damage back to the character performing the move, which of course is the opposite of what is supposed to happen!"

She laughed.

I didn't.

"Whenever something goes wrong," said the woman, "you need to fill out a detailed glitch report."

"There's paperwork?"

"Of course." She nodded toward the clipboard.

It was full of small print.

"Aw man," I said.

"It should take you all afternoon to die everywhere," she said. "But if you finish early, feel free to start running into walls."

"Running into walls?"

"Yes, there is another glitch where the characters keep getting stuck in walls. Which of course ruins the fight."

I couldn't believe this.

"You seem surprised," she said.

"I am," I said. "This is . . . boring."

"But this is what video game testing is," said the woman. "Running into walls and dying over and over again. Good luck!"

She left me in the room.

I put a coin in the machine.

I selected BLUE SPY.

I stood on the first floor by a plant and let RED SPY punch me until stars spun around my head.

Then he used a super move and I died.

The screen flashed:

A timer counted down from a minute.

60...

59...

58...

I put in another coin.

Then I died again.

CHAPTER

29

MORE PAPERWORK

I died over and over again.

I fed the game more coins, and I lost more fights.

I filled out reports for glitches.

The screen went green when I died by the desk on the second floor.

The game froze when I died by the safe in the basement.

And when RED SPY tried to uppercut me on the helipad, the punch knocked him off the roof.

The screen flashed.

"Great," I said.

I filled out a glitch report, played again, and lost.

I decided that I did not want to be a video game tester after all.

My watch beeped.

It was three o'clock!

I slipped quietly into the hall and tried to find the bathroom.

I opened door after door.

Inside each room there were kids sitting in front of video games, the machines making the sad bloops of lost lives or the sharp clicks of hitting walls.

"Sorry," I said. "Just looking for the bathroom."

"Oops," I said. "Just trying to find the bathroom."

"Heh," I said. "I thought this might be the bath-room."

Finally, I found the bathroom.

It was empty.

There was a faint dripping sound from a leaky pipe somewhere behind the wall.

My footsteps echoed off the tiles.

I waited.

I went to the sink to wash my hands, so if anyone came in, everything would look normal.

CHAPTER

30

OK...

I washed my hands for a long time.

CHAPTER
31
LIVE DROP

Finally, a man with long hair and a gray suit entered.

"Hello," he said.

My hands trembled.

"My favorite composer is Mozart," I said.

"Oh!" he said. "I quite adore his Horn Concerto No. 4 in E-flat major."

"Bah!" I said. "I prefer woodwinds, and so enjoy his Oboe Concerto in C major."

The man shrugged.

I blocked the door to the bathroom so he couldn't escape.

"It's you!" I cried. "I got you!"

"I do not understand," said the man.

"I think you do," I said. "Now tell me, what does DRUBBALUBBA mean?"

He looked confused. "DRUBBALUBBA?"

"DRUBBALUBBA!"
Behind me, the door to a stall flew open.
A man was standing up on the toilet.
It was the KGB Man.
He was wearing a shiny red tracksuit.

(At least he was not wearing my jeans.)
"You fool!" he cried. "You brought me the code
yourself! DRUBBALUBBA!"
Oh no.
"Ha ha!" The KGB Man laughed. "Ha ha ha! Look
at you standing there with your mouth open! You look
like a doofus!"

"You look like a doofus," I said. "You're standing on a toilet."

"No," said the KGB Man. "Standing on a toilet is cool. You couldn't see my feet, so you didn't know I was in here!"

"That is pretty cool," said the man in the suit.

The KGB Man jumped down.

Freddie growled.

"When the Queen caught Agent X in London, I thought I would never get the code." He smiled. "But then I realized I could always count on you to mess up!"

"Aw man," I said.

"I left that message in the phone booth for you. The whole thing was a red herring! You played right into my hands!"

"I get it," I said.

"I tricked you!" cried the KGB Man.

"I *get* it," I said.

"Ha!" said the KGB Man.

"You know," I said, "it's really unappealing to laugh at your own jokes."

"Ha ha ha ha ha ha," said the KGB Man.

I folded my arms in front of the door.

"You're not getting out of here until you tell me what DRUBBALUBBA means."

Freddie stood beside me and snapped.

"Good luck getting through us," I said.

"Why do you care?" the KGB Man asked.

"What?"

"Why do you care what DRUBBALUBBA means?" the KGB Man asked. "The Queen put you behind a desk. She gave you a boring job. So you quit. You went rogue. So why are you trying to crack this code?"

I thought about it. "Because the Queen of England asked me to," I said.

The KGB Man sneered. "You could have done whatever you wanted. But ever since you've gone rogue, you've just done what the Queen of England wants."

"Yeah, but not in the way she asked me to," I said.

The KGB Man rolled his eyes.

I shrugged. "I might be a rogue agent," I said, "but I'm still a good person."

"And that is why you will never win!" the KGB Man said.

He put his hands on his waist and laughed at me.

Then he brought his arms forward in a swift and graceful motion.

I thought he was going to perform a devastating attack on my head.

But what he did was even worse.

He tore off the snaps on the sides of his track pants to reveal that he was wearing my blue jeans.

"Aw man," I said.

"Nice spies finish last!" said the KGB Man.

"Great," I said.

"Get it? Normally I believe the expression is 'Nice *guys* finish last.' But I changed it to 'spies.' To be funny."

The man in the suit was laughing.

The KGB Man pointed at him and smiled. "This guy gets it."

Then KGB Man did a backflip out the window.

I ran over and looked out the window, hoping he had twisted his ankle.

But he was crouched like a panther on the cobble-stones.

"Just so you know," I called, "I got it too. I just didn't think it was very funny."

But the KGB Man dusted himself off, hopped on a motorcycle, and tore off down the street, laughing all the way.

I turned back toward the man in the suit.

"Maybe you can help me," I said. "Do you have a car? A fast one?"

The man in the suit smiled at me.

Then he opened the door to the hallway and said, "Security!"

Two guards dragged me and Freddie out to the curb.

I sat there and scratched Freddie's head.

"Well," I said, "I guess that's that."

There was a phone booth on the corner.

It started to ring.

Freddie looked up at me.

"I better answer that," I said.

I entered the booth and picked up the phone.

It was the Queen of England.

"Hello," I said.

"Hullo," she said. "How is life as a rogue agent?"

"Well," I said, "not great."

"I see," said the Queen of England. "And why are you in Japan?"

"I wanted to find out what DRUBBALUBBA meant," I said.

"And did you?"

"No," I said. "I just handed the code off to the KGB Man."

"Ah," said the Queen of England.

"Are you mad?" I asked.

"Yes," said the Queen of England.

"Are you disappointed?" I asked.

"Yes," said the Queen of England.

"Am I demoted?" I asked.

"Demoted?" asked the Queen.

"Yeah. Are you going to punish me?"

"I cannot demote you," said the Queen of England. "I cannot punish you. I cannot do anything to you."

"Just tell me what to do!" I said.

"I cannot give you orders. You are a rogue agent. You are on your own."

She hung up.

I felt awful.

And when I felt awful, I usually played video games to make myself feel better.

(I still do.)

So I sat on the curb and pulled out my Game Boy.

Freddie curled up on my lap.

I rested my Game Boy on his head.

He didn't mind.

He was a good dog.

I flipped the switch.

The screen lit up.

A little bell chimed.

I sighed.

When I was a spy, and when I was a kid, a lot of the time, I had no idea what to do.

But when I played video games, I knew just what to do.

I could turn off the part of my brain that was worried.

The world on the screen became the world in mind.

My thumbs worked the buttons.

Up.

Down.

Left.

Right.

A.

B.

That's all there was to it.

Hit the buttons, at the right time, in the right order.

Down.

Right.

Up.

B.

B.

A.

My score got higher.

I beat the bosses.

I earned more lives.
Left.
Up.
B.
B.
A.
I gasped.
I pressed pause.
I'd cracked the code.

CHAPTER

34

IN FROM THE COLD

I ran to the phone booth, put every Japanese coin I had left into the slot, and called the Queen of England.

"Hullo!" said the Queen of England.

"Hello," I said.

"You have reached the Queen of England. I am unable to come to the phone right now, so please leave me a message at the beep, unless you're a rogue agent, in which case you should hang up right now and have a good think about what you've done. Thank you!"

There was a beep.

"I know what DRUBBALUBBA means!" I said. "Call me back as soon as—"

"Mac, this is wonderful!" said the Queen of England.

139

"Oh," I said. "I thought I was talking to your answering machine."

"No," said the Queen of England. "I was just pretending to be an answering machine because I did not want to talk to you! I made the beep by pressing 9. Wasn't that clever of me?"

"Yes," I said.

"Well?" said the Queen.

"Yes," I said, "it was very clever of you to press the 9."

"Mac," said the Queen, "stop wasting time talking about how clever I am. What does DRUBBALUBBA mean?"

"DOWN, RIGHT, UP, B, B, A, LEFT, UP, B, B, A," I said. "It's a cheat code. For a video game."

"What game?" the Queen of England asked.

"I don't know for sure, but I have a guess," I said.

"SPY MASTER: BATTLE EDITION," we both said at the same time.

"I bet he's going to use it tomorrow, to win the Video Game World Championships in New York City!"

"I bet you're right," said the Queen of England.

"If the KGB Man has a cheat code, Zak doesn't stand a chance," I said. "And the KGB will have its name on the high score list of the entire world."

"Oh dear," said the Queen of England.

"What should I do now?" I asked.

"Isn't it obvious?" said the Queen of England. "Fly to New York City and deliver this code to Zak!"

"Is that an order?" I asked.

The Queen of England smiled.

I could tell she was smiling, even over the phone.

"Yes," she said.

CHAPTER

35

BIG SCREEN

This is Times Square.

Times Square is in the middle of New York City.

For a long time, a newspaper called the *New York Times* had its headquarters there, but it is not a square. It's really more like two triangles, but I think we can all agree that Times Floppy Bow Tie–Shaped Area is not a good name.

Times Square is famous for bright lights and big signs. There are billboards and marquees and jumbo screens.

The screens in Times Square have advertised chewing gum and hamburgers and Broadway musicals.

They are some of the biggest video screens in the world.

So imagine playing SPY MASTER on one of them.

This was the Video Game World Championships in New York City.

Crowds had gathered to watch.

Electric guitars blared.

There was a platform on the sidewalk swathed in smoke from a fog machine.

Atop the platform stood an arcade machine: SPY MASTER: BATTLE EDITION.

Everything that happened on the game was pumped up to the jumbo screen that towered above Times Square.

I arrived, out of breath, and pushed my way through the crowd.

I was nervous about meeting Zak.

I had practiced handing over the cheat code.

I would sit next to him on a bench and pretend to be looking somewhere else.

But I would slide a piece of paper over to him.

"DRUBBALUBBA," I would whisper.

"What?" Zak would say.

"DRUBBALUBBA," I would say. "Use it wisely."

And then Zak's eyes would light up. He would understand.

"Where did you get this?" he would ask.

"From the shadows," I would say. "I work in darkness."

"Wow," Zak would say. "Are you a spy?"

I would smile. But I wouldn't answer.

"Good luck," I would say. "We're counting on you."

And then I would stand up.

"Wait!" Zak would say. "What's your name?"

I would shake my head. "I can't tell you that."

And I would begin to melt into the city.

"But I want to give you a lifetime subscription to *Gamer Mag!*" he would cry out.

And then I would come back and give him my name and address, but I would make him promise to keep it secret.

And he would. And then he would let me touch his spikes.

It was going to be great.

But something was wrong.

The crowd was restless.

There were angry shouts.

A thirteen-year-old kid was standing up on the platform.

He looked like he was about to cry.

Even his spikes looked forlorn.

"Zak!"

But Zak couldn't hear me over the din.

It was horrible.

The KGB Man was standing atop the platform with his arms raised.

A man in a tuxedo was holding a gold medal in the air, ready to hang it around the KGB Man's neck.

A woman in a ball gown leaned into a microphone.

"Announcing the world champion!"

Her voice echoed off the buildings.

I was too late.

SIGH

"What happened?" I asked.

There was a reporter with a notebook standing next to me.

"It's already over," she said. "He beat fifty-four gamers from forty-three countries in less than two hours. I've never seen anything like it."

"He used a cheat code!" I cried.

I rushed to the stage.

I ran up to the microphone. "He used a cheat code!"

Three judges sat at a table next to the platform.

They frowned and shook their heads.

The woman in the gown looked sad.

"We know," she said. "Cheat codes aren't against the rules."

The KGB Man laughed.

I turned and looked up at the jumbo screen. There were tears in my eyes.

RED SPY WINS

WHO WILL CHALLENGE THE CHAMPION?

(INSERT COIN)

The timer counted down.

10 . . .

9 . . .

8 . . .

The KGB Man grabbed the microphone. "I have the high score!" his voice boomed. "The world will know the power of the KGB!"

5 . . .

4 . . .

3 . . .

"Wait!" I said.

I dug into my pocket and pulled out the quarter Craig had given me at the movies.

I dropped it into the slot and slammed the A button.
There was a glorious chime.

CHAPTER

38

A NEW CHALLENGER

The KGB Man rolled his eyes.

"But this kid did not even register for the tournament," he said.

"Arcade rules," I said. "If I've got the quarter, you have to play me."

The judges huddled, then nodded in unison.

"Unbelievable," said the KGB Man.

We selected our fighters.

I chose BLUE SPY.

He chose RED SPY.

The screen flashed, "FIGHT!"

BLUE SPY and RED SPY stood face-to-face on the ground floor of the building.

"I know the cheat code," I said. "But I'm not going to use it."

The KGB Man shrugged.

"OK," he said.

Then, very quickly, he entered the combination: Down, Right, Up, B, B, A, Left, Up, B, B, A.

His character grew three times bigger.

His health bar doubled.

Then a whole second health bar grew beneath him.

His fists started flashing. I didn't even know what that meant, but it didn't seem good.

"Aw man," I said.

I pressed hard on the joystick to make my guy run.

RED SPY chased BLUE SPY around the building.

I crouched beneath desks, which he smashed with his fists.

I tried to hide out in the parking garage. He picked up cars and threw them at me.

On the second floor he cornered me and pressed B for a roundhouse kick.

I was knocked to the ground. My health bar was reduced to a sliver.

I was starting to sweat.

This was not going well.

I took the elevator up to the third floor and pushed a potted plant inside it, so he couldn't use it.

"Can't get me now!" I said.

I had time to punch some orange blocks, which made them turn into pink rutabagas, which I could eat for power-ups. (That sentence probably only makes sense if you've played SPY MASTER.)

RED SPY was stuck down in the lobby. With the elevator stuck up on the roof, there was no way he could hurt me.

Then he did it again: Down, Right, Up, B, B, A, Left, Up, B, B, A.

His character doubled in size.

His shirt ripped.

Then he grabbed on to the side of the building and started climbing it like a tree trunk.

The crowd oohed.

This was terrifying.

I started mashing buttons.

I ran back to the elevator, pushed out the plant, and rode up to the rooftop.

He raced alongside me, scaling the outside of the building and punching his giant fists through the windows.

I reached the roof and stood in the middle of the helipad.

He climbed up to the top and towered over me.

"Nowhere to go now," said the KGB Man.

I tried to duck, but he stomped me.

Stars flew around my head.

I took my hands off the controls.

There was nothing left for me to do.

The KGB Man pressed buttons in rapid fire. It was time for his finishing move. He wound up, and here it came.

A massive uppercut.

The force from the blow sent him flying off the building.

His second health bar vanished.

And so did his first.

The screen went green and froze.

But not before letters two stories tall flashed:

BLUE SPY WINS!

CHAPTER

39

CHAMPION

"What!" said the KGB Man.

"It was a glitch." I shrugged. "You have to know about the glitches."

"He should be disqualified," said the KGB Man. "Disqualify him."

The judges frowned and shook their heads.

The woman in the gown smiled. "Announcing the world champion!"

The man in the tuxedo put the medal around my neck.

The crowd roared.

It took a second to sink in:

I was the Video Game World champion.

CHAPTER 40

THE GLORY OF THE QUEEN

My mom was happy to see me when I got home.
Craig barely looked up from the TV.
"You have some mail," my mom said.
The package on my bed was bigger than usual.
"Oooh," I said.
I read the card first.

DEAR AGENT MAC,
CONGRATULATIONS ON ANOTHER MISSION
ACCOMPLISHED! YOU WILL NOTICE THAT THIS
PACKAGE IS BIGGER than the ONE I USUALLY
SEND as A REWARD foR YOUR EffoRTS. That
IS BECAUSE it CONTains A Box, POSTage paid,
that you may USE To mail YouR FIRST- PLACE
mEdal Back To me. ANY GLORY You AchiEVE in
A TOURNEY IS GIVEN unto ME. JUST LIKE the
KNIGHTS of OLD! Bet you WISH you
HAD STayed A ROGUE agent.
JUST Kidding!
ABout STaying A ROGUE Agent. NOT ABout
SENDing ME the MEDAL. PLEASE DO SO AT
YouR EARLIEST CONVENIENCE.

my MAJESTY,
THE Queen of England
PS: DON'T WORRY! I included a
little something foR you Too!

Before I could unwrap the package, the phone rang.

"I'll get it!" I said.

I got the phone from the kitchen and took it back to my room.

"Hello?" I said.

"Hullo!" said the Queen. "May I speak to Mac?"

"Speaking," I said.

"Did you get my package?" asked the Queen.

"Yes," I said.

"Did you open it?"

"I just got home," I said.

"Wonderful," said the Queen. "I would like to be on the phone when you do."

"OK," I said.

"You know," said the Queen, "I really thought DRUBBALUBBA would end up being a portmanteau. We spent all that time talking about them, for what?"

"Well," I said, "it's always nice to learn something new."

The Queen of England sighed. "I suppose."

I tore off some paper and opened the box.

"Mac," said the Queen, "do you know what red herring is?"

"Yeah," I said. "It's a clue that's not really a clue. Hey, you're right! Portmanteau words were kind of a red herring."

"No, no, no," said the Queen of England. "No. I did not ask if you knew what *a* red herring is. I asked if you knew what red herring is."

"Oh," I said. "No."

"It is an oily fish, salted and smoked till it turns deep red. Over here we call them kippers! Have you ever had a kipper?"

"No," I said.

The Queen let out a squeal. "Look in the box!"

I pulled out a little tin.

"Oh . . ." I said, "my."

"You're welcome!" said the Queen.

I put the kippers in a drawer in my desk, which by now was getting pretty full of things from Britain I would never eat or wear.

"Mac," said the Queen, "I am glad we are getting along again. I suppose a dash of roguishness can be, well, dashing in a spy, but in future missions let's reduce that dash to a pinch."

"OK," I said.

"And I am pleased to inform you," said the Queen, "that the future is now! You see, I need another favor."

I smiled.

THE

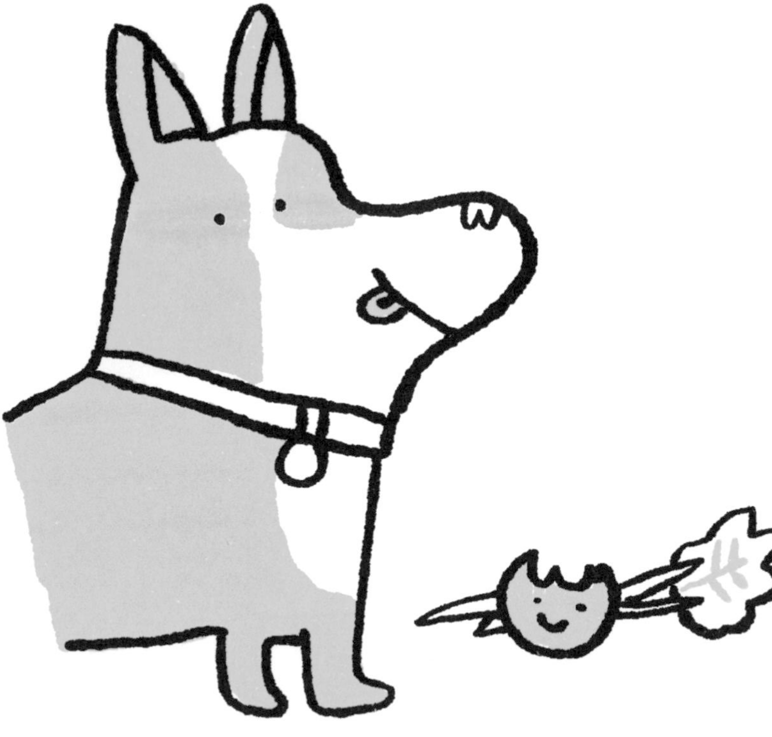

END

Mac Barnett is a *New York Times* bestselling author of children's books and a former ████████. His books have received awards such as the Caldecott Honor, the E. B. White Read Aloud Award, and the Boston Globe-Horn Book Award. His secret agent work has received awards such as the Medal of ████████, the Cross of ████████, and the Royal Order of ████████ ████████ the Third. His favorite color is ████. His favorite food is ████. He lives in Oakland, California. (That's true. You can look it up.)

Mike Lowery used to get in trouble for doodling in his books, and now he's doing it for a living. His drawings have been in dozens of books for kids and adults, and on everything from greeting cards to food trucks. Mike is the author and illustrator of *Random Illustrated Facts*, and the book *Everything Awesome About Dinosaurs and Other Prehistoric Beasts*, with more Everything Awesome series titles to come. Mike lives in Atlanta, Georgia, with a little German lady and two genius kids.

MAC B.
KID SPY

WITH MORE
EXCITING
MAC B.
ADVENTURES
TO COME!